This igloo book belongs to:

....

igloobooks

Published in 2018
by Igloo Books Ltd
Cottage Farm
Sywell
NN6 0BJ
www.igloobooks.com

Written by Melanie Joyce
Illustrated by César Samaniego

Designed by Amy Bradford
Edited by Kathryn Beer

REX001 0418
2 4 6 8 10 9 7 5 3 1
ISBN 978-1-78670-297-5

Printed and manufactured in China

Are we
There Yet?

igloobooks

"Alright," said Daddy. "Go and get ready, the sea is quite a long way."

Little Bear jumped up and down.

I'm off to the sea. Hooray!

Mummy rolled up Little Bear's dolphin towel and put it in his pack.

He stuffed in his bucket and spade, then followed Daddy down the track.

Little Bear raced ahead, as fast as his paws could go.

Daddy laughed and said, "There's a long way to go yet, Little Bear."
But suddenly Little Bear shouted,

I can see the sea over there!

"That's only a stream," said Daddy. "The sea is big and blue. There are noisy birds and sand, and little seashells, too."

Little Bear and Daddy went through the forest and over the hill.

On and on they plodded past squirrels and rabbits until...

Then suddenly they arrived at a big, blue shiny lake.

Then, after a while a tortoise appeared,
carrying a bucket and spade.

That way to
the sea!

You'll see the
sandcastles I made.

KEEP
GOING

Friendly foxes with surf boards, waved and said, "Hello."

Have fun at the sea!

they cried.

It's not too far to go.

Little Bear was terribly excited to think he was getting so near.
But the sandy path went on and on, and the sea did not appear.

Are we there yet?

asked Little Bear.

Daddy, when will it be?

But Daddy just smiled and pointed, because at last they had reached the...

YOU MADE IT!

Little Bear had never seen anything so wonderful before.
He let out a squeal of excitement and ran towards the shore.

All day long Daddy and Little Bear played and laughed together.

Thank you, Daddy,

said Little Bear.

I'll remember this day forever.